[handwritten signatures: Pedro Suarez, Cristina Gutierrez, Janine Romny, Kate Cht., Audrey Eaton, Lauren Groody, Alexandra Dietz, Geraldine Mukumbi]

Stories and illustrations by the children of the Robinson Center
Additional illustrations by Ming Archbold

Produced By: Ming Archbold, Brianna Leon, Sean Fitzgerald, Kara McSweeney, Ann O'Brien, Allison Fachetti, Elizabeth VanKula, Christina Edmonds, Lingyi Li, Brandon Moore, Geraldine Mukumbi, Sarah Senseman, Kelly Keenan, Natia Jones, Kevin Kim, Brian Hartnett

Cover Design: Tanya Alconcel
Front/Back Cover Font: Cabin Sketch, mpallari

Every Child Has A Story
Robinson Community Learning Center

Kameron Austin, Marcus Bowens, Janae Brown, Damaris Buendia, Daniela Buendia, Joshua Crudup, Joseph Habimana, Indonesia Holt, Kai Holt, Ruthie Kiarie, Winnie Kiarie, Haron Kimani, Raelynn Lee, Nathanael Manns, Dylan Maternowski, Imani Miller, Tiana Mudzimurema, Alecia Parker, Alexia Parker, Cameron Pierce, Valencia Randolph, Jordan Rawls, Patrick Rawls, Aniah Williams, and Isaish Williams

Table of Contents

Things We Do at the Robinson Community Learning Center

Marcus Bowen, Daniela Buendia, Joseph Habimana, Haron Kimani, Alexia Parker, Patrick Rawls, Aniah Williams

After school, we go to the Robinson Center, where there are all kinds of clubs, healthy snacks, and games. Our favorite games are Connect Four, Master Mind, Scrabble, chess, Mancala, Hangman, and "Heads Up, Seven Up".

When the weather is nice outside, we play football, four square, jump rope, jackpot, frisbee, and tag.

In Jackpot, the person who's "It" throws a football high in the air and calls out a number. Everybody else tries to catch the football, and if you catch it, you get that number of points. The person with the most points wins!

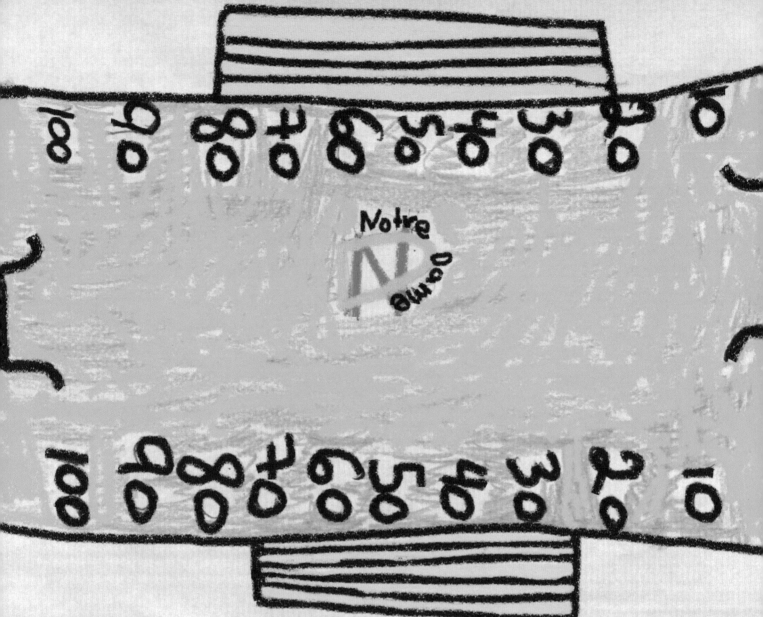

When we play football, we pretend we are Notre Dame players. We have to touch the person with the football with two hands to stop him. At Notre Dame, the field and the players are much, much bigger.

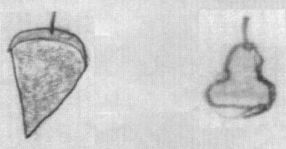

We eat meals and snacks at the Robinson Center. Our favorites are fruits, vegetables, pizza, pretzels, cheese crackers, popcorn, and yogurt.

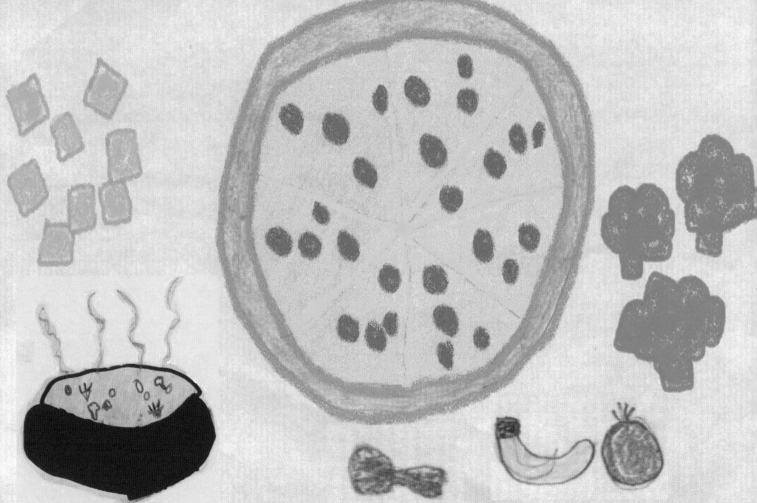

To end the day, we participate in activities like chess club, hockey club, Shakespeare club, and Lego robotics. In chess club, we learn how to use our minds to make wise decisions. The Robinson Center is a great place to learn, and we have fun doing it.

Rock Climbing

Team Shooting Stars: Kameron Austin, Janae Brown, Indonesia Holt, Dylan Maternowki, Tiana Mudzimurema, Alecia Parker, and Jordan Rawls

One day, Mrs. Dorito brought Shaun and Tiffany rock climbing at Notre Dame. Shaun brought his lizard, Stone, along for the adventure, tucked in his pocket. When they got there they met their instructor, Joe.

After putting on equipment, Shaun and Tiffany started climbing on the rock wall. When Shaun was close to the top, Stone climbed out of his pocket and tried to climb up!

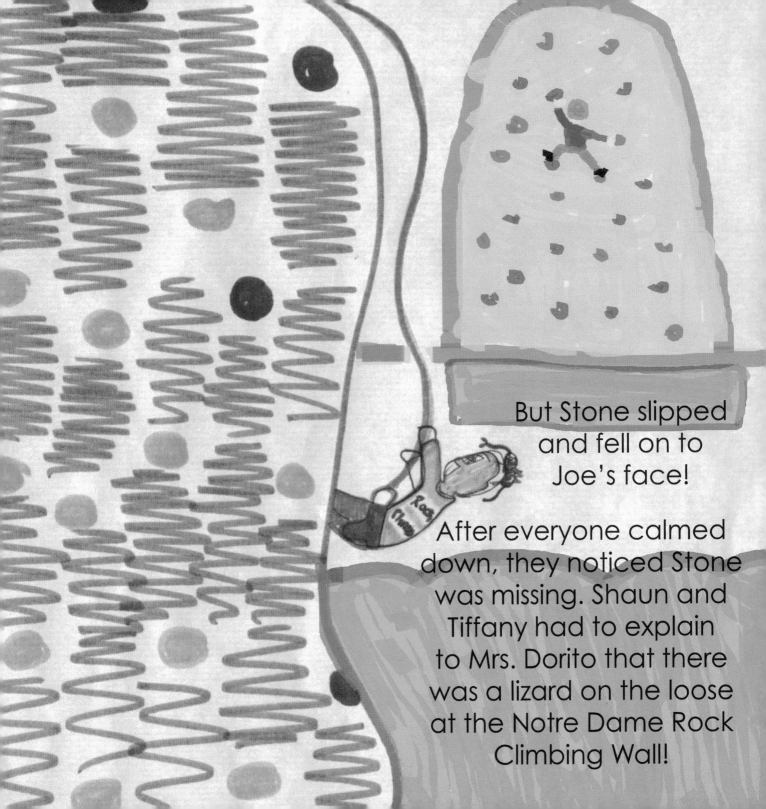

But Stone slipped and fell on to Joe's face!

After everyone calmed down, they noticed Stone was missing. Shaun and Tiffany had to explain to Mrs. Dorito that there was a lizard on the loose at the Notre Dame Rock Climbing Wall!

Everyone went on a wild goose chase for Stone.

They checked the basketball courts, the racquetball room, and even the bathrooms.

But despite their teamwork, they couldn't find Stone. Everyone got in the van and started driving, hoping they would find Stone.

All of a sudden, Stone jumped out of Mrs. Dorito's pocket and onto the window! Mrs. Dorito screamed. Shaun and Tiffany just laughed.

Everyone was happy that they found Stone and they headed back to the Robinson Community Learning Center. They learned never to give up hope, even when things seem lost.

Brian the Great

Cameron Pierce, Ruthie Kiarie, Winnie Kiarie,
Valencia Randolph, and Isaish Williams

It was a monday morning, and as usual, Brian had overslept. "Get up sleepy head!" shouted Brian's mom.

He came downstairs to eat a nutritious breakfast. But as he was eating, he heard the roar of his school bus...

He
ran
outside
and...

...fell in a big
puddle of mud!

But he got up and kept running, determined
to catch the bus. Just as Brian was about
to give up, the bus suddenly stopped and
splashed mud on him.

Embarassed, he jumped on and everybody laughed at him. Luckily, Samantha, the girl Brian likes, told him to sit next to her. He got very nervous, but quickly felt better because Samantha asked him to study with her for that week's history test. They were learning about the Revolutionary War.

After school that day, Brian went to Samantha's house to study the Revolutionary War. They acted out a battle, with Brian as a Patriot soldier and Samantha as a British soldier. Brian wore old clothes with lots of holes and Samantha wore a nice red coat that was neat and clean.

They moved the battle outside and pretended that it was a long and cold winter. Brian wanted to give up, but General Washington's passion for independence gave Brian stength. Finally, after hours of swordfighting, Samantha was defeated. Brian was free! He ran around Samantha's room waving the American flag and cheering.

At school the next day, Brian was very nervous for his test. But he remembered his play date with Samantha and knew it would help him remember the Revolutionary War. When their teacher gave back the tests a few days later, Samantha and Brian were happy to find an A+ on both of their papers! They both agreed that American history is fun to learn.

The Trip

Damaris Buendia, Joshua Crudup, Kai Holt, Haron Kimani, Raelynn Lee, Nathanael Manns, and Imani Miller

One day, we were enjoying our time at the Robinson Center like we usually do after school. Our group was in the middle of snack time when Mrs. Velshonna came in the room and announced that we were going on a field trip to Washington D.C.! We were all very excited to go because President Obama lives there!

The next day, an airplane flew us to D.C. and we arrived at a very crowded airport. As we walked around the airport, we daydreamed about seeing the White House and all the other attractions in D.C. Then, out of nowhere, a rush of people separated our group from Mrs. Velshonna! We walked outside to look for her and spent hours searching, but it was getting dark out and we were afraid that we would never find her. Frightened, we were walking down a dark street when, all of a sudden, we saw a flashing light...

It was the headlights of a limousine! The driver pulled up next to us and asked, "What are you kids doing out here?" "We are lost!" we fearfully responded. So the driver started chatting with someone in the car and, suddenly, the car window rolled down. Slowly, it was revealed that the person in the car was the president!

President Obama asked us with a smile on his face, "Why don't you guys hop in the limo?" Surprised, we all looked at each other and hopped in. We were all astonished by the President's kindness.

When we reached the White House, the first lady opened the door and introduced herself and her daughters.

We were all so happy to meet the president's family! Michelle then took us on a tour of the White House. It was so big that, once we finished the tour, it was time for dinner. We were all very hungry and we had a lot of laughs with the president's family over the delicious meal.

After dinner, the president took us to where we would sleep, but we realized we weren't tired. So the president told us we could hang out in the basement. He brought us to an elevator where there was a big painting of George Washington on the wall. He turned the picture frame sideways and typed a password on the picture. All of a sudden, the elevator made weird noises and took us deep underground...

As the doors slowly opened, a huge lab with many potions, gizmos, and gadgets was revealed! We were all amazed and looked around the huge lab. Then, we all spotted a huge colorful water fountain. Thirsty, we ran to the water fountain to have a drink.

"Oh no!" shouted President Obama. But we didn't hear him so we started drinking. All of a sudden, our stomachs started grumbling and our bodies were shining brightly. Then, "Poof!", we all turned into superheroes!

"Now you know the secret to my powers!" said the President. "Come and help me prevent divorces, feed the hungry, give money to the poor, lower the gas prices, and stop bullying in schools." We were all excited but a bit afraid of the large task.

It seemed impossible to solve all of these problems, but we realized the President needed help. So day after day, we moved from state to state, doing all we could to help our fellow Americans. We transported food to soup kitchens, broke up school fights, and even gave counseling to married couples.

But there were a lot of people who needed help. Solving all the problems of America was very difficult. It felt like months, but one morning, we woke up and something had changed. Where did our superhero suits go?

Then, it all hit us...

We never went to the lab and got super powers. We all fell asleep as soon as we got to our beds! It was all a dream...

But, even though we weren't super heroes, we realized we could still help solve the problems of America. It was our passion and diligence that aided us, not our powers. And even though we could only help out in small ways...

We knew that even kids like us can make a difference.

Eventually, we said our goodbyes to the Obama family and thanked them for taking care of us. The Obamas also gave us a farewell, and just as we were driving through the exit gates of the White House, President Obama shouted, "You have some problems to solve, my little helpers!"

Made in the USA
Charleston, SC
04 May 2013